BOOK CLUB
IN A BOX

Bookclub-in-a-Box presents the discussion companion for Andrea Levy's novel
Small Island

Published by Review, an imprint of Headline Book Publishing, London, 2004. ISBN: 0-7553-07518

Quotations used in this guide have been taken from the text of the paperback edition of **Small Island**. All information taken from other sources is acknowledged.

This discussion companion for **Small Island** has been prepared and written by Marilyn Herbert, originator of Bookclub-in-a-Box. Marilyn Herbert. B.Ed., is a teacher, librarian, speaker and writer. Bookclub-in-a-Box is a unique guide to current fiction and classic literature intended for book club discussions, educational study seminars, and personal pleasure. For more information about the Bookclub-in-a-Box team, visit our website.

Bookclub-in-a-Box discussion companion for Small Island
ISBN 10: 1-897082-36-3
ISBN 13: 9781897082362

BOOKCLUB-IN-A-BOX

Andrea Levy's Small Island

BOOKCLUB-IN-A-BOX
Readers and Leaders Guide

Each Bookclub-in-a-Box guide is clearly and effectively organized to give you information and ideas for a lively discussion, as well as to present the major highlights of the novel. The format, with a Table of Contents, allows you to pick and choose the specific points you wish to talk about. It does not have to be used in any prescribed order. In fact, it is meant to support, not determine, your discussion.

You Choose What to Use.

You may find that some information is repeated in more than one section and may be cross-referenced so as to provide insight on the same idea from different angles.

The guide is formatted to give you extra space to make your own notes.

How to Begin

Relax and look forward to enjoying your bookclub.

With Bookclub-in-a-Box as your behind the scenes support, there is little for you to do in the way of preparation.

Some readers like to review the guide after reading the novel; some before. Either way, the guide is all you will need as a companion for your discussion. You may find that the guide's interpretation, information, and background have sparked other ideas not included.

Having read the novel and armed with Bookclub-in-a-Box, you will be well prepared to lead or guide or listen to the discussion at hand.

Lastly, if you need some more 'hands-on' support, feel free to contact us. (See Contact Information)

What to Look For

Each Bookclub-in-a-Box guide is divided into easy-to-use sections, which include points on characters, themes, writing style and structure, literary or historical background, author information, and other pertinent features unique to the novel being discussed. These may vary slightly from guide to guide.

INTERPRETATION OF EACH NOVEL REFLECTS THE PERSPECTIVE OF THE BOOKCLUB-IN-A-BOX TEAM.

Do We Need to Agree?

THE ANSWER TO THIS QUESTION IS NO.

If we have sparked a discussion or a debate on certain points, then we are happy. We invite you to share your group's alternative findings and experiences with us. You can respond on-line at our website or contact us through our Contact Information. We would love to hear from you.

Discussion Starters

There are as many ways to begin a bookclub discussion as there are members in your group. If you are an experienced group, you will already have your favorite ways to begin. If you are a newly formed group or a group looking for new ideas, here are some suggestions.

Ask for people's impressions of the novel. (This will give you some idea about which parts of the unit to focus on.)

- Identify a favorite or major character.

- Identify a favorite or major idea.

- Begin with a powerful or pertinent quote. (not necessarily from the novel)

- Discuss the historical information of the novel. (not applicable to all novels)

- If this author is familiar to the group, discuss the range of his/her work and where this novel stands in that range.

- Use the discussion topics and questions in the Bookclub-in-a-Box guide.

If you have further suggestions for discussion starters, be sure to share them with us and we will share them with others.

Above All, Enjoy Yourselves

INTRODUCTION

Suggested Beginnings

Novel Quickline

Keys to the Novel

Author Information

INTRODUCTION

Suggested Beginnings

1. Small Island is a novel about some big themes found in current literature – for example, racism, intolerance, and bigotry. Levy's perspective comes from the stories of individual people and their history. She is interested in cultural conflicts from the points of view of all who are affected.

Into what category would you place Levy's novel? Consider the factors presented in the book – intolerance, courage, cultural environment, education. Are there other factors that could be included?

2. Levy uses humor rather than drama to show racial tension between the blacks and the whites in her novel. The story of the segregation of black American GIs was a true situation that Levy found through her research. The British had no idea or experience in dealing with this form of racism, so they tried to accommodate all requests.

Compare British and American racism as it is presented by Levy. Did she succeed in portraying the evils of bigotry with her humor?

3. Levy has structured this novel around four narrative voices, each of which represents a different aspect of the social divide.

Are these voices balanced? Does one voice stand out from the rest, and why? Who do you think is Levy's favorite or most interesting character?

4. The adjective "small" plays a significant role in Levy's novel because it not only describes the two islands – Jamaica and Britain – but it addresses the people, their dreams, and their perspectives. In addition, many of her characters are physically small.

Consider all sides of this concept in relation to the themes and the characters in the novel.

5. Levy feels that the immigration process not only changes those who have immigrated to a specific country, but it also profoundly affects the people who have accepted those same immigrants into their midst.

Discuss this idea in light of the characters presented in this story.

6. Queenie's baby is life's circle complete and brings together the past and the future.

Is this ending satisfactory and/or optimistic? As a mother, how can Queenie give up her child? Has she made a reasonable decision to ask Gilbert and Hortense to raise her baby? Consider the implications of each character's response to this issue, including Bernard's.

Novel Quickline

Small Island is the delightful story of Jamaican immigration to post-war Britain in the days before England's predominantly white population began to show a visibly different demographic profile. While England was struggling to get back on her feet, she was suddenly overwhelmed by an influx of loyal Jamaicans and other colonials who had fought on Britain's behalf during the war, alongside Britain's own servicemen. Using their British passports, they returned to England in 1948 because their own homelands were even more economically depressed than England. They were certain that their "mother country" would welcome them and would gladly reciprocate the help now that they were in need. We are introduced to four narrators – two British-born, two Jamaican-born – who each tell the story from his or her own perspective.

Jamaican Gilbert Joseph is one of the ex-RAF pilots who returns to England on the ship, *Empire Windrush*, followed by Hortense Roberts, his hastily acquired Jamaican wife. Both Gilbert and Hortense have always been sure that their love and reverence for the "mother country" would ensure an open-armed welcome. Gilbert spends the six months prior to Hortense's arrival living in small, cramped quarters in a room in Queenie's boarding house. Circumstances are not what he had imagined, and he spends his time just trying to keep a low profile in his job as a postal driver so that he doesn't attract negative and prejudiced attention. His grim discovery of racism and his consequent disappointment precede what Hortense will certainly experience soon after her arrival.

Kind-hearted, gentle Gilbert tries hard to soften the blow to Hortense's pride and sense of identity, but Hortense Roberts is a pompous, self-centered Anglophile, and we quickly see that she is headed for a fall. The scenes depicting Hortense's reaction to her new home, her new husband, and her new landlady are some of the funnier scenes of the novel.

Queenie, wife of Bernard Bligh and daughter-in-law of Arthur (all white, native Britons) is Gilbert's alter ego. She is as color-blind as Gilbert when it comes to people in need. Gilbert had helped her out during the war, and when he arrives post-war looking for a place to live, she returns the favor. They have a fine relationship until the arrival of Hortense and the surprise return of Queenie's missing husband, Bernard, two years after the war's end. Both Hortense and Bernard offer the black-and-white face of prejudice and intolerance, a contrast to the humanity and acceptance shown by Gilbert and Queenie.

There is a surprising twist at the end of the novel, guaranteed to open the discussion of prejudice as it has been presented by Levy.

Keys to the Novel

Voices

- The novel has four narrative voices: a young black man, a young black woman, an older white man, and an older white woman. Through them, Levy looks at cultural conflicts from all sides and tries to give each voice equal size, weight, and time. These are the people who live out the questions of class, race, and empire building. As we listen to her characters, we become aware of how each voice changes and fluctuates in size and stature, as each character comes up against obstacles in his or her path.

Compassion and Respect

- In this book about racial prejudice, intolerance, misconception, and stereotype, Andrea Levy uses a refreshingly gentle and nonjudgmental touch. Without bitterness or anger, Levy brings to life both the real people who create the intolerance and those who are affected by it.

- Levy's own parents emigrated to England from Jamaica, so she has witnessed firsthand the courage and dignity of people who choose to start anew in another country. These immigrants often face unforeseen challenges, including racism, in environments that can be hostile and ignorant of who they really are. While she intends her story as a tribute to the brave dreams and stoicism of her parents, her other purpose is to honor all people on both sides of the immigration story, because for both the native citizens and the newcomers, life becomes irreversibly changed.

- Levy's primary focus is not to explain the face of racism but to portray the faces of the individuals determined to forge new lives in a positive way, even when confronted with the indignities and outrages of racial prejudice. In a small way, this novel is a contrast to the more turbulent emotions and behaviors seen in the world today. Levy has said she is saddened to see the anger that accompanies these behaviors, but she recognizes that the world is very different now from the one she portrays in 1948. (see Summary, p.63)

Irony   ... *the communication of language*

- There is much humor and irony in the novel, but the absolute final irony is language. Everyone speaks English, but no one understands anyone else. Think of the opening chapter when Queenie attends the British Empire Exhibition; the streets of London where Hortense desperately tries to communicate; the army bases where the senior officers refuse to hear what Gilbert is saying, and the disbelief of the American black soldiers as to what they are hearing Gilbert say. We laugh at these scenes, but there is a disturbing truth to their message about communication that Levy is putting forward for consideration.

- Andrea Levy adds an additional dimension of nonverbal communication by describing Gilbert's habit of sucking his teeth, which was a cultural expression of relief and celebration. Gilbert was quite distressed at the order to not suck his teeth. He viewed this as a complete denial of his right to articulate his feelings. *"Now ask an Englishman not to suck his teeth and see him shrug. Tell a Jamaican and see his face contort with the agony of denied self-expression."* (p.113)

Author Information

- Levy was born in England in 1956 to immigrant Jamaican parents. Like her other three, this novel contains a great many biographical facts of her family and other families like them. Her mother, whose real name is Hortense, has accused Levy of "thieving" their personal history and turning it into fiction. In reality, her parents never talked much about their past because they were always too busy working to keep their family comfortable. Levy's father passed away more than twenty years ago, and her mother is still hesitant to bring up all that "ancient history," mostly because she is not comfortable with the spotlight in which Levy is basking. Like all mothers, she is looking to protect her child. She feels that though Levy is currently enjoying national and international attention through her writing, she may one day be disappointed.

- The youngest of four children, Levy grew up in council housing (rented and subsidized). Her youth was uneventful, filled with television, music, and a mixture of friends, both white and black. Her original ambitions included acting, but mostly she drifted into her career choices. She studied textile design at art school and worked as a fabric designer and buyer of textiles. This led to her working in the BBC and Royal Opera House wardrobe departments. It was in this period that she met her husband, Bill Mayblin, a graphic designer. They have been together for close to twenty-five years, but they were married only a few years ago.

- Growing up as a black child in Britain, Levy maintains that her early social experiences did not include the shame of being black that is felt more profoundly today. In fact, she defines herself as British, not black. Her novel emphasizes that although racism did exist, her family's response to it allowed them to grow and live well. She had few discriminatory shadows on her happy childhood. Nevertheless, her parents did try to teach her to do what Gilbert tries to do – *"[to] keep her head down"* and not attract attention.

- Curiously, Levy was not a reader when she was growing up. She couldn't see the point of books when television was so readily available. Reading the works of Dickens, Bronte, and Austen was only relevant to her as a school experience and was not meant for pleasure. She has clearly changed her opinion since then, and her love of reading includes the novels of such diverse authors as George Eliot, Philip Roth, and Kazuo Ishiguro.

- The book that changed her perspective on reading was, interestingly, Marilyn French's **The Women's Room**, a book she read when she was twenty-three years old. Newly addicted to reading, she searched for novels about her own British-based, cultural, and racial history, but all she could find were books written by African-American writers who were looking for their own particular commonality. So she became a writer herself.

- She did not enjoy immediate success because publishers at the time were not interested in black British writers, thinking that the readership might be too small. When she did finally get published, she was moderately well received. But her success became even more pronounced once writers like Zadie Smith (**White Teeth**) and Monica Ali (**Brick Lane**) came on the scene. Levy credits Smith, in particular, with making black writing mainstream.

- The three novels written prior to **Small Island** all have biographical elements: **Every Light in the House Burnin'** (1994), a semi-autobiographical story set in London in the 1960s; **Never Far from Nowhere** (1996), a 1970s story of two sisters living on a London council estate; and **Fruit of the Lemon** (1999), the tale of a young black woman who visits Jamaica and discovers her unknown personal history.

- Although **Small Island** won the Orange Prize in 2004, the Whitbread Prize and the Commonwealth Writer's Prize in 2005, her mother's fears about the spotlight were prophetic. Levy, who so definitely identifies herself as British first, was shocked to see that the shortlist for the Orange Prize had only one British writer on the list – Rose Tremain. "*It hurt me to think I am not regarded as British; I felt an outsider.*" (Gerard) But a recent announcement hopefully makes up for it: **Small Island** has won the "Best of the Best of all the Orange Prizes" for the last ten years.

- Of all her novels, **Small Island** specifically explores the history of the British-Jamaican connection, which is usually buried as a footnote in history books. She uncovered these footnotes to her personal history when she went to Jamaica for the first time in 1989. There she discovered a whole slew of relatives about whom she had known nothing. For example, her mother's great-grandfather was a red-haired Scotsman, while her great-grandmother was born a slave.

- Her father's father was a Jew who married a black woman and converted to Christianity while he was fighting in World War I, just as Gilbert describes his own father's story. In fact, everything we know about Gilbert's identity and his biographical history conforms to Levy's personal information. The novel opens in Britain and is the place where Levy begins her search for identity.

- While studying and researching Jamaican history, Levy realized that her father and his twin brother came over on the *Empire Windrush*, and so she began the four-and-a-half-year process of writing this book. **(see How Gilbert and Hortense ..., p.22)** Her mother, like Hortense, had followed her father six months later. Her parents had both been very much of the mindset of coming "home" to the mother country in search of a better life, and, like Gilbert and Hortense, they were shocked at what they found.

- Again like Hortense, Levy's own mother had been a teacher in Jamaica but had to take a sewing job (just as our Hortense will) in order to get by. The real Hortense Levy did go back to school, received her teaching degree in England, and eventually retired with the status of deputy head teacher. Levy's father remained a post-office clerk. Despite their hardships, her parents always spoke kindly of the people who took them in (for example, the "Queenies" that they met). The intense racial tensions in the country now make Levy quite sad.

BACKGROUND INFORMATION

British Empire Exhibition

British Empire

Jamaican Experience

Jamaican – Jewish Connection

Decline of the Empire

Gilbert and Hortense to Britain

BACKGROUND INFORMATION

British Empire Exhibition

- The novel opens with Queenie's childhood visit to the British Empire Exhibition, a scene that sets the stage for the unfolding of events and characters in the novel. Here we get a deep sense of the strong and dysfunctional relationship between Britain and those countries in her care.

- The British government's purpose behind the exhibition was to strengthen the bonds between the mother country and her "offspring" and to stimulate trade. It was to enable all who owe allegiance to the British flag to meet on common ground and learn to know each other. (This is Gilbert's cry.) This exhibition was held at Wembley only twice: in 1924 and 1925. Nearly all the countries of the empire participated at the time, sending people and goods, just as Queenie describes it.

- From the opening scene, we see that the British people are quite unaware of the peoples under the control of their empire. Through Queenie, we witness the dignity shown by the commonwealth participants on display and the indignity of their treatment at the hands of the British visitors to the exhibition. In this and later scenes, Levy magnificently captures the voices and attitudes that Gilbert and Hortense would have faced as blue-collar workers in the England of that time.

- For those readers planning to visit Great Britain, there is an excellent exhibition called *Empire and Us* at the **British Empire and Commonwealth Museum in Bristol.** Details can be found at www.empiremuseum.co.uk/.

British Empire

- For a couple of centuries, Britain literally and figuratively owned the world. She began collecting territories, protectorates, and colonies in 1783. It was only the years between 1945 and the early 1980s that saw the empire finally and completely crumble and fall. All that remains is an association of loyal countries that form the commonwealth. Currently there are fifty-three commonwealth countries. At the height of British power, around World War I, Britain held control of approximately one-quarter of the world's population – 500 to 600 million people in over a hundred countries.

- Britain saw herself as the cream of civilization, a model for everyone, the biggest and the best. In the opening scene, the maid and boyfriend, who accompany Queenie and her family to the exhibition, demonstrate their version of British civility: he pees behind the bush; she tries to amuse herself by forcing Queenie to kiss the African Prince. The dignity belongs to Queenie and the Prince.

- The British empire was the uncontested power that gave the world English as the international language of commerce and communication. English was taught in schools throughout the world as a means to build and maintain the empire. With education as the unification tool, the British could convert and conquer. Many of the colonial countries, especially in Africa, the Caribbean, and the South Pacific, had only informal systems of education in place. They also had been under the control of other countries for so long that they had no official record of their own history. Therefore the British were able to step into the vacuum with help from the churches and missionaries.

• The British were often warmly welcomed, since the colonies saw this education as their key to achieving "white-man's" success and as the means by which they could come to understand the white society that was now firmly in control of them. A common language created the appearance of a common culture.

The Jamaican Experience

• As Levy's story opens, Jamaica has had virtually no history free of foreign domination. In 1655 Britain captured Jamaica from Spain, which had in turn taken it from the Portuguese. The use of slavery, a Portuguese creation, was adopted by Britain as a useful and lucrative institution in its colonies. During the seventeenth and eighteenth centuries, Britain traded goods in Africa for slaves, who were then sold in America and the West Indies. In the end, the British were responsible for transporting two and a half million African slaves to the New World, in addition to the four million slaves already in place from the Portuguese.

• The reasoning behind the concept of slavery is as follows. All New World empires needed a reliable and strong workforce. The indigenous peoples of the islands were dying of disease imported from Europe, and the Europeans themselves were unsuited to the climate. The Africans were the ideal answer because they were excellent and skilled laborers in agriculture, cattle management, and in the mines. In addition, they were resistant to tropical diseases and were already comfortable in a hot climate.

- When slavery came to an end in the mid-1800s, the British needed to find new ways to continue the growth of British culture and values as a means of keeping countries like Jamaica connected to the empire. This is where the education of the masses came in handy. An overwhelmingly English atmosphere was created for the benefit of the ruling class, one that promoted the illusion of creating a better life for the native inhabitants, socially and economically. The local people were enthusiastic because they looked forward to the equality promised them.

- In actual fact, the education system denied the native populations any real opportunity to change their socio-economic position. There were different levels of schooling, as is illustrated in the story, and in this way, the British split the society and widened the gap between the haves and have-nots. In doing so, they were able to develop and keep any economic gains in their own hands or in the hands of a chosen few.

- Despite the inequality, the education system promoted an ideology that meant that West Indians became more connected to Britain than to Jamaica. The country was simply overwhelmed by too much British influence that lasted for too long. As a result, it is easy to understand Gilbert and Hortense's attachment to, and their expectations of, the "mother country."

Jamaica and the Jewish Connection

- The Jews were one of the first ethnic groups to settle in Jamaica, because they came to the Caribbean and Guyana first with the Portuguese in the late fifteenth century and later with the Spanish. They came to escape religious persecution, but because they had skills in sugar manufacturing, they were able to help establish sugar plantations, which have become a mainstay of the Jamaican economy.

- When the Spanish left and the British took over, many of these Jews chose to stay and were encouraged to do so. They flourished under the British and were given tremendous freedoms for the simple reason that they increased the numbers of the white population. They were a small, but influential group. Gilbert represents the Jewish presence through his white Jewish father.

- The Jewish population reached its height in the late 1800s, numbering about 2500. Today, the population hovers between two hundred and three hundred.

The War and the Decline of the British Empire

- It was after World War II that British global influence began to decline. The British were having a rough time with German superiority on the seas. Eventually, the Allies definitively won the German war, but it was the other war front, the Japanese-Asian war, that exposed the weaknesses and vulnerabilities of Britain and her empire.

- In 1942, just after the attack on Pearl Harbor, the Japanese launched a major and successful offensive against the British. The Japanese bombed Singapore, where the British were stationed, purging the Chinese population and executing many of the British officers. The prisoners they took were forced to work (often to death) on building the Burma railway, known as the death railway. (This is the story of the famous bridge portrayed in the 1957 movie *The Bridge on the River Kwai*.) In February of 1942, the British surrendered to the Japanese, but the war continued until America defeated Japan three years later.

- In Calcutta, the British were still in control when riots broke out in an effort to provoke political independence. Thousands were killed, and the British needed to maintain order. The war depleted Britain's military resources and emotional will to continue ruling an unruly Empire. Calcutta and Burma were the troubled areas that Bernard entered.

How Gilbert and Hortense came to be in Britain

- As members of the Commonwealth, Jamaica's sons, comprising a force of tens of thousands including five thousand Royal Air Force (RAF) volunteers, joined the British armed forces. All were proud to wear the British uniform. Jamaica had not yet begun to clamor for its own independence. (There is a hint of this at the beginning of the story, where Hortense meets Gilbert in the market, the day a riot breaks out. The speaker that day was Alexander Bustamente, who eventually went on to become Jamaica's first president.)

- During the last days of the war, skilled and unskilled Jamaican labor was needed, and both the U.S. and Britain actively recruited in Jamaica. One hundred thousand Jamaicans had entered America in 1943, and others, who were not already army volunteers, went to Britain. While the doors to the U.S. shut at the end of the war, they did remain open in Great Britain, since these commonwealth members carried British passports.

- The arrival of the *Empire Windrush*, which landed in Tilbury, England, in 1948 with five hundred ex-British Jamaican servicemen, is credited with being the moment that changed the British color landscape forever. In actual fact, Britain had been a multicultural society for centuries. There were very tiny pockets of blacks, with larger groups of Jews, Dutch, and other eastern Europeans, all of whom were considered "bloody foreigners."

- With the arrival of a significant number of people of color, Britain witnessed a new racial dynamic in the country. Where earlier white immigrants had succeeded, the blacks did not do so well because of the discrimination against them – low key, understated, but definitely present.

- When the *Windrush* landed, very few of the immigrants intended to stay permanently in Britain. The Jamaican ex-servicemen came mostly out of economic necessity, because things in Jamaica were very bad. Others came along simply for the adventure.

- The fact that the Jamaicans had British passports facilitated their passage to England but did not mean that they were welcomed by the British. There was evidence in places like Birmingham (one of several cities with a large black population) of this type of message on the Rooms to Let signs: *"Sorry, no coloureds, no Irish, no dogs."* Various laws were put in place that tried to make it more difficult for immigrants to enter the country, but it was recognized that *"these people have British passports, and they must be allowed to land ...There's nothing to worry about, because they won't last one winter in England."* (Birmingham.gov.uk) This is a sentiment echoed in the novel.

CHARACTERIZATION

Gilbert

Hortense

Queenie

Bernard

Arthur

Michael Roberts

CHARACTERIZATION

Each of the four main characters has a distinctive and delightful voice. Levy's first career choice was acting, so it is not surprising that as she wrote each character's section, she play-acted the characters in her head. Levy admits that as she composed Hortense's dialogue she sat at the computer wearing Hortense's hat and white gloves. It's a lovely image. It would also not surprise readers to know that a dream come true for Levy would be to meet her characters and enjoy their company. Gilbert is her favorite, but Bernard is her most fascinating character. Levy feels he is multilayered and she would like to really understand him better.

Levy's success is that her characters are balanced against each other and fully composed. Each is confident in his and her individual assumptions or myths about him or herself and the world, even when those assumptions are challenged. Each is forced to rise, or fail to rise, to whatever occasion occurs. Levy shows them in full-surround, warts, flaws and all.

Gilbert

- Gilbert Joseph is a half-black, half-Jewish, Jamaican-born volunteer to the British RAF during World War II. Before he enlisted, he tried to make ends meet through the schemes of his cousin Elwood. Gilbert is well intentioned, easygoing, and fun loving. With the exception of his abandonment of Celia, Gilbert is a warm, compassionate, moral human being. According to the name books, Gilbert means "trusted," a fitting description for this character.

- During the war, he meets Queenie through a series of odd events and helps her out with her father-in-law, Arthur. When he comes back to England and has trouble finding a place to stay, Queenie returns the favor and gives Gilbert a room in her boarding house.

- Gilbert has been raised as a true and loyal colonial son, whose love for Britain is never challenged. When Britain is in trouble during the war, Gilbert (and others like him) answer the call and join as volunteers.

- Gilbert explains his motivations to Elwood. He tells how Hitler has issued edicts that identified Jews and Blacks as anthropoids. When Gilbert looks up the meaning of anthropoid, he discovers this description: *resembling a human but primitive, like an ape.*

  > *Two whacks I got. For I am a black man ... I was ready to fight this master race theory. For my father was a Jew and my brother is a black man. I told Elwood, "If this war is not won then you can be certain nothing here will ever change."* (p.109)

Although his loyalty is initially challenged by his wartime experiences, it is only once he is back in England after the war that Gilbert becomes truly disenchanted with what he finds.

- His agonizing question, *"How come England did not know me?"* hangs over the novel and forms a challenge to Gilbert's lifelong assumption that his efforts and sacrifices for England would be recognized. Gilbert is a victim of unrequited and unanswered love on more than one level. He grows to understand his new reality, that he is an outsider looking into British society. Two things allow Gilbert to function more productively than Hortense: a) Gilbert survives his disappointments more successfully because of his more relaxed personality; and b) his relationship with Queenie gives him the assurance that at least one native of the "mother country" sees him as he is.

Hortense

- Hortense has always been sure and confident that as the daughter of the legendary Lovell Roberts, she would be recognized and respected for her name alone. She is prim, proper, and protected by the myth with which she has surrounded herself. She is the village snob, a perspective based solely on her renowned but missing father and her light-colored skin.

- Hortense is intensely driven and ambitious, and although both Jamaica and England are hierarchical societies, she is comfortable with such a structure because she perceives herself to be superior. However, neither her ambition nor her snobbery can help her in her professional efforts, either at home or abroad. What she hides from everyone, but most importantly from herself, is the fact that the circumstances of her birth were every bit as illegitimate as those surrounding Queenie's baby. When she applied for a position at a prestigious school in Kingston, the headmaster was *"concerned not with [her] acquired qualifications but only the facts of [her] upbringing ... [her] breeding was not legitimate enough for him to consider [her] worthy of standing in their elegant classrooms before their high-class girls."* (p.71)

- Hortense is a victim of unrequited love in the real sense. She has loved Michael Roberts her entire life but is so consumed by her emotions that she cannot see what is in front of her nose. Sadly for Hortense, Michael Roberts looks everywhere for love, except to her.

- Hortense stands high up on a "proud-and-haughty" ladder and from there looks down on everyone, especially on Gilbert and Queenie. This position leaves her vulnerable to a great fall, like Bernard. Hortense eventually comes to appreciate Gilbert's strength and kindness and to feel compassion for Queenie. She is the character who grows the most. Because she softens and accepts her reality, she is able to move forward.

Queenie

- Queenie is truly a queen befitting of the title, notwithstanding the roots of her upbringing. She is gracious, kind, and respectful of most people. Queenie is the protector and nurturer of her immediate family, especially Arthur and even Bernard.

  > There I was, protecting my husband against those big bad incendiaries, that nasty flying shrapnel, and the horrid, horrid bombs from the naughty, naughty German planes. (p.226)

  Bernard is childish despite his physical size, and he is the only child she ends up keeping. (see Suggested Beginnings, p.7)

- Queenie is as color-blind as Gilbert. She has few illusions or expectations of anyone and so is the most content of all the characters. She accepts whatever comes her way and handles every situation with dignity and consideration. She has always been pragmatic and realistic about her personal position and prospects and is the most farsighted in terms of her son's future and potential reality. Sadly, she is the one character who loses the most in the end.

- Queenie and Bernard represent the conundrum of British society – open on one hand and closed on the other.

Bernard

- Bernard has trouble speaking directly to anyone, a result of his mother's teaching that good boys are to be seen, not heard. He does not present a good British face, and in fact we see him mostly through Queenie's observations of the back of his neck. This interesting image tells us that Bernard is both fearful and rigid. Fear can be hidden on a face, or even in the eyes, but the hairs on the back of a neck will usually give it away. The term "red neck" fits Bernard accurately. His prejudiced outlook is reflected in his customary unexplained response to Queenie when he says, *"I've got my reasons."* (p.217) He usually has no reason that he can elaborate.

- Bernard is a foolish and bigoted man, but he is not all bad. He does redeem himself at times, through his love for Queenie and in his relationship with Maxie. But in the meantime, Bernard suffers from the illusion of supremacy. He is so confident in his England as a white, Anglo-Saxon country that he does not need much prompting from his bigoted neighbor, Mr. Todd, to adopt and spout racist attitudes.

- Bernard is every bit a product of his empire-driven society as are Gilbert and Hortense. British history has taught Bernard that Britain owns the world and so, by extension, does he. Despite his experiences in India and Burma, Bernard has not gained any understanding or humility about Britain in relation to her colonies. Both Britain and Bernard's worlds have changed and are changing, and Bernard simply cannot keep up.

- Levy gives Bernard's original surname as *Blight*, from which the "t" was dropped, making it *Bligh*. The name change was supposed to change the family's luck, but it didn't work. Levy uses this interesting name because it has both a literary and a historical connection. There was a Captain William Bligh who transported a tree called the breadfruit from Tahiti to the Caribbean (including Jamaica) as a cheap source of carbohydrates for the slaves. The breadfruit is a large, round, starchy fruit, usually baked and roasted, but not very flavorful.

- The same Captain Bligh, however, was a victim of a mutiny in the South Pacific. Bernard, too, was involved in the mutiny in India. Bernard is the clearest character representation of the British empire. Both are complex and ambivalent by nature. We know that the British empire failed; we can assume that Bernard will not be very successful in the future.

Arthur

- Arthur is Bernard's shell-shocked World War I survivor father, a man whom Bernard looks after loyally but does not know. Arthur returned home from the first war without words or reactions, and neither Bernard nor his mother ever pushed him to recover. Their care of him was automatic and mechanical, not caring or sensitive.

- It takes Queenie to look at Arthur as a person and not as a victim. She thinks of him as an apostrophe mark, which she was taught in school meant that something was missing. *"... that was how I'd always seen Bernard's father, Arthur: a human apostrophe ... to show us that something precious had gone astray."* (p.238) Queenie gradually learned to read Arthur's face, especially his hairy and expressive eyebrows. They developed a lovely relationship of mutual love and respect. Arthur is far from the useless person that Bernard thinks he is.

- Bernard is posted overseas, and under Queenie's sunny warmth Arthur begins to *"unfurl as sure as a flower"* no longer shaded by Bernard, the overbearing tree. It is Arthur who gives Queenie permission to take in boarders. For Queenie, Arthur becomes a war-time magician, bringing home food and even a potential lover. One day, Arthur surprises Queenie by actually speaking. After Queenie's near-fatal injury in a bombing incident, Arthur gently cares for her and tells her, *"'I would die if anything happened to you,' he said, one careful word at a time."* (p.254)

- It is Arthur who also gives her permission to love. Acutely observant, Arthur knows that Queenie has slept with Michael Roberts. When Arthur sees Gilbert, who has already been acknowledged by Hortense as having a breathtaking resemblance to Michael Roberts, he brings him home to Queenie. Gilbert is Arthur's gift.

> *"Oh, I know why he followed you," she said. "He thinks he knows you. He brought you back for me."*
> (p.141)

Michael Roberts

- Michael Roberts has been the love of Hortense's life since childhood. They lived and played together in the house where Hortense was taken by her grandmother to live. Although related to the Roberts family on her father's side, Hortense's grandmother, Jewel, became their servant, and Hortense, until she and Michael were grown, were playmates.

- When Michael Roberts first went off to boarding school and later to the army, Hortense was devastated. *"Squeezing my nails into my hand until blood pricked on my skin. I did not want to cry ... I had been told, when there is too much pain, tears nah come."* (p.35)

- Always the adventurer, always the playboy, Michael Roberts finds warmth in the arms of the white women he encounters: first, with Mrs. Ryder, *"the whitest woman ... her short blonde hair sat stiff as a halo around her head"* (p.37), and later with Queenie. Michael Roberts seems to have followed in the footsteps of his cousin, Lovell Roberts, Hortense's father. Both are ladies' men, and both become absentee fathers.

- Michael Roberts's resemblance to Gilbert is so strong that when Hortense first sees Gilbert she chases him through a crowd of demonstrators. Gilbert rescues her after she falls.

> *... he placed me gently down and I saw his face. It was him. It was the man I thought was Michael. But it was not Michael. It was a stranger.* (p.68)

Ironically, Hortense wonders where in the world Michael Roberts could really be, when all the while he was traveling the same path as Gilbert, just a few steps ahead. Like Gilbert, Michael Roberts boards with Queenie for a few days. Charming as ever, Michael Roberts has an extraordinary effect on her.

> *... Mrs Bligh usually worked out what she could make for dinner during sexual relations with her husband. But this woman, if it hadn't been for the blackout, could have lit up London.* (p.248)

FOCUS POINTS
AND THEMES

Identity

Small Island

Prejudice

Patriotism

FOCUS POINTS AND THEMES

Andrea Levy is not investigating the big themes of racism, intolerance, or bigotry that often consume other fiction, but she certainly doesn't shy away from them. She is most interested in ordinary people and their stories. She looks at them within the framework of immigration – those who come to a new place and those who take them in. Both sides become changed in the process, and Levy is curious about the strategies these people devise in order to live together side by side. Some strategies are big; some are small. People's ideas, hopes, dreams, and perceptions take on a different validity when juxtaposed against the ideas, hopes, dreams, and perceptions of others.

Identity

- A look at the theme of identity must include a look at the immigration process as it existed then. Levy first establishes how each character sees him or herself and considers the influences that have formed their self-perceptions. From there she moves on to focus on the process of interaction between all these different people. Finally, she concentrates on the idea that immigration is a process that changes everyone – both the immigrants and the community that receives the immigrants. Levy uses her own family as a model and was herself changed by the experience of researching this book. She admires what the immigrants experience and what the British themselves went through during the war. Both sides had a similar coping strategy – pick yourself up and keep moving on.

- Each of the characters feels larger or smaller depending on where they are, what they are doing, and with whom they are in contact. In their respective pasts, they are all quite certain of their identity and their place in their community. But this identity can change as the environment changes and according to how others see them. As a result, there can be a confusion of identity and, in some cases, the bursting of a character's personal mythology.

- Levy uses the concept of size (large and small) as a descriptive device. The novel's title, **Small Island**, is a metaphor for the shifting nature and perspective of each character's identity.

  o Gilbert, the handsome boy in blue, perceives himself to be as British as his fellow RAF fighters. Sadly, Gilbert comes to realize that the only perception others have of him is as Gilbert the driver for both the air force and the post office. Nowhere to be seen is Gilbert, the lawyer: a dream that he hopes Britain will give him the opportunity of attaining.

  o Hortense sees herself as a gift to the education system. She is certain that England will allow her to shine and to show herself as a dedicated product of the British system. When she applies

for a job as a teacher, she is so undermined by people's inability to understand her King's English and by their refusal to grant her an interview that she blindly walks through the first door she sees – into a utility cupboard. Already threatened by the reality of life in England, Hortense is further embarrassed and reduced in status.

o Bernard is so tall that he can see clearly over the heads of those around him and as a result he often forgets to look down to see who his neighbors are. His self-perception is that he is "Britain" and everyone else is an interloper. He goes off to fight in the war so that he can be a hero to Queenie. However, Bernard, the hero, is nowhere to be found: not in London, nor in Burma. No matter how much of the big world he encounters, he continues to see things and people as small. Ironically, he is perceived to be small, despite his height.

o The real Queenie is also different from her perception of herself. Although she is very accepting and democratic, she is perceived by the Mr. Todds of the world as a dangerous person who singlehandedly ruins society and as a queenly, dignified, and giving personality by Gilbert, the reader, and by Arthur. Although she takes exception to Mr. Todd and Bernard's perceptions of her, she is too modest to allow herself to be puffed up by the perceptions of others.

• Tied to identity is the theme of recognition. There are many cases of mistaken identity; for example, there are the times when Gilbert is mistaken for Michael Roberts. Levy herself questions whether it is possible to get the recognition we deserve. This is a personal issue for her, especially in light of her experience as an Orange Prize nominee. (see Author, p.11)

Small Island

- Levy is intrigued by how people who come together from different backgrounds and from different cultures can manage to live peacefully side by side. They bring with them dreams, perceptions, and memories of different sizes, and they may have come from smaller or larger places than where they have come to settle. The title then has many overlapping thoughts, some obvious and others not.

- Levy uses the physical size of her characters to point out these differences. Both Gilbert and Hortense are perceived to be physically bigger than they really are, yet we are told that Gilbert is shorter than Bernard, and shorter still than the American GIs with whom he comes into conflict. Hortense is even smaller than Gilbert, and this has its challenges. But because Gilbert is an attractive and commanding personality, he appears to be tall. Hortense seems bigger simply by virtue of how much she puffs herself up. Even though we are told that Bernard is tall, he is shortened by his many insecurities. Queenie, herself, is a tall and regal woman. In this way, Levy drives home her point on perspective, which properly belongs in the eye of the beholder.

- Size is also connected to dreams and hopes, and we watch as the big hopes and dreams of the characters are crushed or at least cut down in size.

  o In Jamaica, it is the other surrounding islands that are referred to as small islands. Jamaica itself is the largest of the English-speaking islands but by no means the largest of the Caribbean islands. After the war, when the men returned from England, they were suddenly confronted with Jamaica as a very small island. (see Fast Facts, p.61)

o Likewise, Bernard and the other British soldiers returned from overseas to the realization that their once large place in the world was shrinking, leaving them with only their small island as the center of their existence.

o After living in England during the war, the Jamaicans who returned to their mother country were also faced with how the big island had shrunk in stature due to their treatment at the hands of the British. It is the relativity of place and identity that shocks both groups and is reflected in the four characters, who despite their connections to each other are individually their own small islands.

Prejudice – British/American Style

- Levy sees the racism in Britain, both during and after the war, as being fundamentally different from the racism in the United States. At the time this story takes place, segregation in the United States was pronounced and supported in some places by law. In Britain, by contrast, there were not many people of color, and their presence was not yet an issue that had to be addressed, despite the fact that bigotry did exist.

- In her research for the novel, Levy came across newspaper accounts that she fictionalized into the scenes involving the American soldiers in the restaurant and in the movie theater. Britain had no firm segregation policies in place, but the Americans in Britain demanded that something be done to keep black and white soldiers separate from each other. One solution was to designate whole towns as being open to blacks and to whites on different days. What the Americans were not prepared for was the number of black Jamaican army personnel who wandered freely throughout the country. As a result, there were reported tales of West Indians being harassed by white American soldiers and street fights between the two groups. Levy realized at once that the West Indians were fighting the war on two fronts.

- The British were uncomfortable with these solutions, not because racism did not exist – it did – but because American racism was so overt.

- Everyone needs to picture the face of the enemy in order to fight effectively. For Gilbert, his declared enemy is the American soldier who cannot stand to see a black man who holds his head up and doesn't know his place. *"If the defeat of hatred is the purpose of war, then come, let us face it: I and all other coloured servicemen were fighting this war on another front."* (p.147)

- But all of this is not to say that British racism did not exist. Gilbert comes to it head-on in his job. He is stronger than his fellow workers and could easily beat them up, but *"what else could this Jamaican man do? I dropped my head."* (p.262) He goes on with his work, because what matters most to him is keeping his job. (see **Author Information, p.11**)

Patriotism, Loyalty, and Master Race

- Britain went to war because she was threatened by Hitler's aggression. Hitler wanted to construct an empire built on the idea of a master race: one that would control all others. Britain had previously succeeded in building an empire, based on the ideas of British superiority, economic savvy, education, and civility. There is, of course, one major difference: Hitler was prepared to wipe out an entire people and culture by murder; Britain attempted to change entire populations by changing their perspectives, allegiance, and culture through education and economic control. However, it must be acknowledged that British domination has caused considerable hardship and, in some cases, destruction of existing societies and cultures. (See **British Empire Exhibition, p.17**)

- Both Gilbert and Bernard go to war for the same reason – to protect and preserve the world they know and love. They wear the same uniform. Each looks at it with fierce loyalty and each is fully prepared to defend it. When Queenie looks at Gilbert, she sees the same boy *"... in the RAF, a boy in blue fighting for this country just like Bernard ..."* (p.97)

- Although they seem to be fighting the same enemy, these two faces of patriotism are not considered equal by others, certainly not by Bernard. Gilbert is looking to prevent his beloved society from becoming divided by the black and white faces of prejudice. Bernard is looking to keep those very same faces in his beloved society separate from each other. *"... it was the darkie woman I saw first. What a sight! On our street. Never seen that before. I was dumbfounded to see that the white woman she accompanied was Queenie."* (p.353)

- For Bernard, the recipe for life is each to their own.

  The war was fought so people might live amongst their own kind. Quite simple. Everyone had a place. England for the English and the West Indies for the coloured people ... Everyone, except these blasted coloured colonials. I've nothing against them in their place. But their place isn't here. (p.388)

- Gilbert's love of England matches or supersedes Bernard's.

  Let me ask you to imagine this. Living far from you is a beloved relation whom you have never met. Yet this relation is so dear a kin she is known as Mother. Your own mummy talks of Mother all the time ... Her photographs are cherished, pinned in your own family album to be admired over and over. Your finest, your best, everything you have that is worthy is sent to Mother as gifts. And on her birthday you sing-song and party. (Queen Victoria's birthday is still celebrated annually in Canada and in other commonwealth countries.)

Then one day you hear Mother calling – she is troubled, she need your help. Your mummy, your daddy say go, Leave home, leave familiar, leave love ... Soon you will meet Mother.

The filthy tramp that eventually greets you is she. Ragged, old and dusty ... no smile, no welcome. Yet she looks down at you through lordly eyes and says, "Who the bloody hell are you?" (p.116)

All Gilbert ever wanted was to be a hero to Britain, recognized for his love and loyalty. All Bernard ever wanted was to be a hero to Queenie. Their dreams are different sizes, but both return to an England shrunk and withered.

- It is not a great leap from the discussion of patriotism to the discussion of what Gilbert describes as the master-race theory. The British empire was built around the concept of "master servant," a relationship that is so eternal and ongoing in the world and in history that novelists are constantly asking if it can ever change. It is an especially fitting and ironic theme in this novel. Britain was fighting a war against Hitler's Germany, a regime that epitomized for all posterity the idea of a master race. Bernard, Gilbert, and the American GIs all went to war to fight against this idea of bigoted control. Levy makes a loose parallel, not a comparison, and she does it through the use of irony.

  o The Americans go to war to fight Hitler's practice of racial aggression, but they came from a situation of racial discrimination both at home and abroad.

  o Bernard begins his fight with Hitler but is then moved on to the South Asian arena to fight against Japanese aggression. Meanwhile, his whole outlook is colored by the fact that he enlisted to fight for the purpose of maintaining the status quo, social and racial purity, at home.

o Gilbert comes to the RAF without ever having experienced out-right discrimination in Jamaica. He simply answers a call of need. But he certainly understands Hitler's position against "blacks (anthropoids) and Jews," because he is both. Sadly and ironically, he learns about prejudice far from his home, both from the British and from the Americans. These encounters and conversations are pointedly funny.

... I was ready to fight this master race theory. For my father was a Jew and my brother is a black man. I told Elwood, "If this war is not won then you can be certain nothing here will ever change." (p.110)

Now, from what I could understand, this American officer ... was telling us that we West Indians, being subjects of His Majesty King George VI, had, for the time being, superior black skin. We were allowed to live with white soldiers, while the inferior American negro was not. I was perplexed. No, we were all perplexed. (p.110)

WRITING STYLE AND STRUCTURE

Narration

Language

WRITING STYLE AND STRUCTURE

Narration

- Each of Levy's narrators is a distinctive and individual voice. This is quite a literary accomplishment. Each character speaks for him and herself, and through their voices the reader understands their strengths, their weaknesses, their prejudices, and their perspectives. Through their interaction, Levy gives us a photograph of time and place.

- The result is alternately heartwarming or disturbing, but always informative. We learn about the big and small differences in culture, in experience, in compassion, and in perspective.

Language *humor and irony*

- Levy captures the nuances of language in the individual voices of Gilbert, Hortense, and the other Jamaicans, with the musical dialects they use when they talk among themselves, as opposed to the stiffer dialogue we hear when they speak to others. Therefore, we wince when Hortense asks Queenie, *"This is perchance where [Gilbert] is abiding?"* (p.10) Hortense is intensely proud of her King's English and puts her best verb forward.

- Miscommunication is always humorous in a novel and is especially so in the exchanges that Gilbert has with the two black American soldiers. The humor in their exchange is gently mocking but clearly shows the potentially deep and hurtful emotions of both the soldiers and Gilbert. The two young soldiers, Jon and Levi, were impressed by meeting Gilbert, but, like others, they had no idea where in the world Jamaica could be found. They find it mind boggling to hear Gilbert say that he is British, but not English, that he is from Jamaica but England is his mother country.

    "Joe, I don't altogether understand what you're saying. Jamaica is in England and who is your mother?" Levi asked.

    "Well, Joe, I think I get it now. This island, Jamaica, is in the Caribbean Sea." Jon nodded, pensively turning to his friend. They understood. *"So,"* Levi carried on, *"the British have all their black folks living on an island. You a long way from home just like us."* (p.131, 132)

The American boys can only see things in terms of their personal experiences and how they are seen in their world. They cannot understand that a black man like Gilbert might have a different experience.

- Levy's use of language is exceptionally auditory. We can hear the Jamaican "cha" and the sucking of the teeth loudly and clearly an act of expression that for Jamaicans is as necessary as breathing. For the American sergeant, it is an act of subordination.

We also hear their thoughts as clearly as if they had been spoken aloud.

> ... every action we took confirmed to this man [American sergeant] that all West Indian RAF volunteers were thoroughly stupid. Eating, sleeping, breathing in and out! Cor blimey, all the daft things we darkies did. We did not know that answering the question "What is it, Airman, kill or be killed?" with the answer, "I would prefer to kill you, Flight Sergeant," would see you up to your neck in bother. (p.113)

- Gilbert is not upset by racist language, such as "colored," "black," or "nigger." It is the word "soldier" instead of "airman" that is the greatest insult. The other words he can deal with because he is black by color. To be called a "soldier" is to attack the essence of his dreams and identity. This is a much more serious issue.

- There are a number of funny one-line statements in the story, spoken especially by Gilbert.

> Did people think I was lost on my way from the canefield? (p.132)

> Laughter is part of my war effort. (p.143)

> Meanwhile those GIs were concentrating on us like we were an exam they must pass. (p.148)

> The GIs were blocking the door. I needed a plan. It was too late to don a disguise – they would still know me in a blond wig. (p.150)

SYMBOLS

Airplane, Ship

Duality

Trunk

SYMBOLS

Levy's symbols are not complex or even subtle, but she presents them in such a lovely way that they must be mentioned. The reader can sense the fun Levy had in presenting them.

Airplane, Ship

- The airplane and the ship are vehicles, the means by which one gets from one place to another. With these vehicles, Levy takes us to different levels of meaning. Levy lets her themes circle and finally land. To make another analogy, she floats her ideas from herself to the reader. In addition to these modes of transportation, Levy also includes travel by donkey and by truck.

- The different voices and the time changes are the different themes looking for a place to land. When Gilbert tries to communicate with the black American soldiers, he wonders *"whether anything I was saying was going into his head or merely circling around it searching for somewhere solid to land."* (p.132) Likewise, the ship cutting through the waves is Levy cutting through the racial and cultural myths and stereotypes in order to better present them. Hortense herself is like a ship, slow to turn and change direction.

- If the route to understanding the story's themes is not clear enough from the journey across the water, Levy also takes her characters (and her readers) by truck over land. The donkey may represent the stubborn characters who need time to digest the subtleties of the reactions they get from others in this novel.

- As has been said in Keys, p.10, Levy is delicate in the treatment of her themes. She allows the reader to reach informal and personal conclusions, quickly or slowly, by whatever means the reader wishes. Levy makes no judgments, only presentations.

Duality

- There are parallels and juxtapositions everywhere in the story. First, there are two couples, on either side of the color divide, who have the same hopes, dreams, and concerns about identity and love. Next are two men, both of whom support Britain in her hour of need, but neither of whom receive that same support when needed. Then there are two women, in love with the same man, each of whom will be mother to the same baby. Duality strongly supports Levy's main idea that there are always two sides to everything; it just depends on your perspective.

- In Jamaica, as a teacher, Hortense came across a set of twins ... *"two boys, Leonard and Clinton looked so alike I puzzled on the need for both of them to exist."* (p.72)

- Kenneth and Winston are also twins who physically symbolize the concept of duality. Initially, Gilbert has trouble telling them apart but eventually comes up with a system to identify who is who. Kenneth is the one who constantly asks for money; Winston always offers help. In fact, Winston demonstrates the "pardner" system (see Last thoughts, p.62) and offers Gilbert a job as superintendent in a rental house he has purchased. This job allows Gilbert and Hortense to live there, fix the place up, and rent out the rooms to others.

    > *Winston was my cavalry. He rode in at my hour of need.* (p.415)

Trunk

- One of the more humorous images in the book is Hortense's trunk, which of course is the literal baggage she brings with her to England. The actual items that we are told are inside do not account for its heaviness and bulkiness. The only items we see come out of the trunk are Hortense's wedding dress, a very lovely and colorful blanket from home, and some food items. We have to assume that the rest of the weight comes from her emotional baggage.

    > *[Gilbert and Kenneth] Silly as two pantomime clowns we struggled with this trunk – but at a steady pace. That is, until the trunk fell back down one whole flight when Kenneth, letting go, insisted that a cigarette – which I had to supply – was the only thing that would help him catch his breath. How long did it take us to reach the room? I do not know. A fine young man when we start, I was a wheezing old crone when we eventually get to the top. And there is Hortense still sitting delicate on the bed, now pointing a white-gloved finger saying, "You may place it under the window and please be careful."*
    >
    > *Kenneth and I, silently agreeing with each other, dropped the wretched trunk where we stood, just inside the door.* (p.19, 20)

LAST THOUGHTS

Fast Facts

"Pardner" System

Summary

LAST THOUGHTS

Fast Facts *(2004 census information)*

- England's population is 50 million; Great Britain, as a whole, has 60 million. The size of the island is 245,000 square kilometers (or approximately 98,000 square miles).

- Jamaica's population is 2.5 million on an island of 11,000 square kilometers (4,411 square miles).

- Approximately 90 percent of Great Britain's population is white (including English, Scottish, Irish and Welsh), while only 2.3 percent of the population is black. There is an overwhelming Christian majority.

- About 90 percent of Jamaica's population is black. While the majority are Christian, 34 percent of the population is made up of Rastafarian and other non-Christian denominations.

- The median age in Jamaica is 26, and the literacy rate is over 87 percent.

- The original Jamaicans migrated north from South America in the years from 1000 BC to 400 BC. They were gentle people, most likely Arawaks or Tainos. These indigenous people died out through contact with the Europeans, who brought disease. This began with the Portuguese, who were already in the Caribbean and South America.

- In 1494, Columbus claimed the island for Spain, and the Spanish made slaves of the natives. One million people were wiped out within fifty years, requiring the Spanish to find a new source of cheap labor. Following the Portuguese model of bringing slaves from Africa, the Spanish did the same.

- Britain captured the island from the Spanish in 1655 and continued the successful slave trade. Cotton grew wild on the island, but the major export became sugar, an enterprise made successful by the presence of the Portuguese Jews who came to the new world in the mid-1500s to escape persecution in Europe. (see Jamaica and the Jewish Connection, p.20)

"Pardner" System

- As the Jamaican immigrants (and likely others from the Caribbean area) began to arrive in Britain in the forties, fifties, and sixties, they set up their own institutions and organizations, since they were excluded from many that already existed. One of these institutions was the "pardner" system, a co-operative method of saving and sharing money. Participants would contribute to a weekly "kitty" and then take turns using the proceeds to buy property.

- Winston uses this means to purchase his first and subsequent houses.

> ... *some of the boys from his district back home start a pardner. He have a little saving so he join them. His turn soon come round for the hand. Now with this and some money his grandma give him from selling her land to a big-time movie star, he find he have enough to buy a house. Here, in London ... the place need fixing up a bit, which was the reason he could purchase it at a preferential rate.* (p.413)

And, of course, this is where Gilbert comes in handy. *"'I wan' you come fix up the place, Gilbert. You can come live there with your new wife. Other room we board to people from home. No English-woman rent. Honest rent you can collect up. And then you see the place is kept nice.'"* (p.414)

Summary

- Levy maintains that her books are not about race but about individual people and their history. (see Keys, p.10) She looks at them introspectively, in a positive, inquisitive, and absolutely nonjudgmental manner. However, she does acknowledge, mostly through Hortense and her experiences, that there are levels of superiority even among Jamaicans. The lighter the skin, the more privileges were available. Equally true, especially in Jamaica, is that privileges and benefits were given to loyal supporters of Britain and the monarchy. These details are threaded throughout the story and are an example of how Levy clearly shows the flaws of her characters but is sympathetic to them nevertheless.

- While Levy claims that she did not experience overt racism in her younger years, she explains that there were things she chose to look at from a different perspective. She talks of the odd days when her friends would stop talking to her because she was black, but the next day, they were back knocking at her door. These incidents never cast any shadows on her happy childhood. Her mother would also say from time to time that people would call her *"'darkie,' but then of course, I was dark."* During her teaching days, Levy's mother had the occasional parent request that a child be removed from her class because she was a black teacher. But from her perspective, she felt she got the better deal – these children were often troublemakers and she was glad to be rid of them. It is ironies such as these, learned from her parents, that are evident in Levy's writing style. (see Author Information, p.11)

- **Small Island** is a tightly woven novel, despite its apparent simplicity. Levy's major themes and keys that drive the novel are bound up with her writing style, structure, and imagery. For example, the main themes of identity and the relativism of perspective, which is beautifully represented by the idea of "small island," relate to each other and add to the reader's understanding of both concepts. Her stylistic use of different narrative voices enriches the themes. The different chapters, each representing a different character, add to the sense that the characters do not, and cannot, have a complete picture. Levy drives home the point that empathy and a positive outlook are important to one's personal ability and willingness to see things from another point of view. Levy's use of humor lightens the serious issues while revealing the nature of miscommunication. We laugh with and appreciate the characters without scorn or ridicule.

- Levy is saddened by the tensions that currently exist in her England and by the pressure put on young black teens, especially the young men. Levy believes that police scrutiny and racism based on skin color create a self-fulfilling prophecy, one that she doesn't see as being successfully handled or avoided in today's society. The novel **Small Island** is Levy's attempt to remind us that things good and bad come out of our own personal perspectives and it is there we have control. Given the way things are in many countries at the moment, let us hope that people take her message to heart.

- Levy gives the last word to Winston Churchill as a reminder that a few people *can* change things.

> *Never in the field*
> *of human conflict has*
> *so much been owed by*
> *so many to so few*

Winston Churchill

(see novel, p.439)

FROM THE NOVEL

Quotes

FROM THE NOVEL...

Memorable Quotes from the Text of Small Island

PAGE 9. I did not dare to dream that it would one day be I who would go to England. It would one day be I who would sail on a ship as big as a world and feel the sun's heat on my face gradually change from roasting to caressing. But there was I! Standing at the door of a house in London and ringing the bell. Pushing my finger to hear the ding-a-ling, ding-a-ling. Oh, Celia Langley, where were you then with your big ideas and your nose in the air? Could you see me ... in London? Hortense Roberts married with a gold ring and a wedding dress in a trunk. [Hortense}

PAGE 22. ... this is a tricky meter. Sometime it smooth as a piggy-bank and sometime it jam. Today it jam. I have to stand back to give it a kick so the coin will drop. But, oh, no, one kick did not do it. I hear her demurely sucking on her teeth at my second blow. How everything I do look so rough?

When I light the gas fire again I say, "Take off your coat, nah?" And victory so sweet, she finally do something I say. Mark you, she leave on her little hat and the blessed white gloves. I had no hanger for the coat. "You wan' a cup of tea?" I say. I had been meaning to get another hanger – the only one I have has my suit on it ... I go to throw the coat on the bed, but I am no fool, just in time I hang it over me suit instead. [Gilbert]

PAGE 41, 42. With love it is small signs you have to look to ... All the world knows teasing is a sign. And [Michael] liked to tease me with his learning, urging me to test him on all the capital cities of the world. Australia, New Zealand, Canada.

... "Test me on my knowledge. Ask me of the League of Nations or beg me explain the Irish question."

He knew I knew nothing of these, but boasting to impress had been used since Adam first looked upon Eve. [Hortense]

PAGE 56. And all girls classified as astute were given the honour of entertaining everyone at evening assembly with a recitation ...

... I was the talk of the college for several weeks. And when I thought my spirits could go no higher, my fairy cakes – with their yellow cream and spongy wings – were declared by the domestic-science teacher, Miss Plumtree, to be the best outside the tea-shops of southern England. [Hortense]

PAGE 59. Marching in disciplined rows through the streets that afternoon, these men, dressed entirely in thick blue cloth, looked as uniform and steely as machinery ... this fighting machine was merely composed of line after line of familiar strangers. Fresh young boys who had only just stopped larking in trees ... Big-bellied men who would miss their plantain and bammy ... It seemed all the dashing, daring and some of the daft of the island walked there before me.

So many men.

"Why must so many go?"

I thought I had spoken these words only in my head but Celia, facing me somberly, replied, "You must understand, if this Hitler man wins this war he will bring back slavery. We will all be in chains again. We will work for no pay."

"Celia, I work for no pay now," I said, thinking of my worthless class.

Perhaps she did not understand my joke ... I could understand why it was of the greatest importance to her that slavery should not return. Her skin was so dark. But mine was not of that hue – it was the colour of warm honey. No one would think to enchain someone such as I. All the world knows what that rousing anthem declares: "Britons never, never, never shall be slaves." [Hortense]

PAGE 83. It took Gilbert only two hours to decide to ask me if I would marry him. And he shook my hand when I said yes, like a business deal had been struck between us. [Hortense]

PAGE 86. Then, for the first time, he kissed me gently on my mouth. His breath smelt of rum but his lips were warm and soft against mine. I closed my eyes. When I opened them again he kissed me once more but this time the man poked his wet slippery tongue into my mouth. I choked finding myself sucking on this wriggling organ ...

Turning away, I took off my hat to place it delicately in the cupboard. I could have been no more than five seconds but when I turned back Gilbert stood before me as naked as Adam ...

... "Keep that thing away from me!" I said.

"But Hortense, I am your husband." He laughed, before realising I was making no joke. The fleshy sacks that dangled down between his legs, like rotting ackees, wobbled. If a body in its beauty is the work of god, then this hideous predicament between his legs was without doubt the work of the devil. [Hortense]

PAGE 96. But two years went by and no Bernard or any word from him. All the men had come home. They were back walking round the streets, chatting in pubs, courting on park benches, riding on buses, taking all the blinking seats on the tube. The War Office swore blind they'd returned Bernard. I made an appointment to see them and a self-important little man stared at me with pity in his eyes. He's left you missus, he's left you, his look said. But they didn't know Bernard Bligh. He wouldn't do anything half so interesting. [Queenie]

PAGE 105. ... every last one of us was too preoccupied with food ...

This was war. There was hardship I was prepared for – bullet, bomb and casual death – but not for the torture of missing cow-foot stew, not for the persecution of living without curried shrimp or pepper-pot soup. I was not ready, I was not trained to eat food that was prepared in a pan of boiling water, the sole purpose of which was to rid it of taste and texture. How the English built empires when their armies marched on nothing but mush should be one of the wonders of the world. [Gilbert]

PAGE 108. "... while you are at this military establishment ... and guests of the Government of the United States of America you will have the run of this camp. Everyone here has been ordered to see that your stay with us is the best welcome Uncle Sam could give to the negroes of an ally." He was shouting now. "You will mix with white service personnel. Have you boys any idea how lucky you are? You will not be treated as negroes!" [Gilbert]

PAGE 154. "Madam, there is no Jim Crow in this country."

"Who?"

"Jim Crow."

"Well, if he's coloured he'll have to sit at the back."

"Segregation madam, there is no segregation in this country ... This is England, not Alabama."

... My heart thumped so I feared the toe-tapping beat would be told to shush. Cha, nah, man – is bareface cheek! We fighting the persecution of the Jew, yet even in my RAF blue my coloured skin can permit anyone to treat me as less than a man. [Gilbert]

PAGE 172. "... why so many young men and women queuing up for passport? Why so many striking for job and busting up the place? Elwood, I have seen it with my own eye. The world out there is bigger than any dream you can conjure. This is a small island. Man, we just clinging so we don't fall off." [Gilbert]

PAGE 177, 178. ... still breezy from the sailing on the Windrush these were the first weeks for we Jamaicans. And every one of us fat as a Bible with the faith that we would get a nice place to live in England – a bath, a kitchen, a little patch of garden ... Two months ... I needed somewhere so I could start to live.

So how many gates I swing open? How many houses I knock on? Let me count the doors that opened slow and shut quick without even me breath managing to get inside ... If I had been in uniform – still a Brylcreem boy in blue – would they have seen me different? Would they have thanked me for the sweet victory, shaken my hand and invited me in for tea? Or would I still see that look of quiet horror pass across their smiling face like a cloud before the sun, while polite as nobility they inform me the room has gone? [Gilbert}

PAGE 204, 205. "Queen B," that was what Father started calling me. He like to tell everyone about the day Queen B fainted in the butchering shed at the sight of blood ...

After that I became a vegetarian. "A what?" Father thundered at the table, "A ruddy what?" Who'd ever heard of that? A butcher's girl who won't eat meat. A blithering turnip head ...

It was not long after I'd shouted at my dumbstruck father that Aunt Dorothy came to visit. Mother's posh sister from London, who pronounced her aitches with a panting breath even when there were no aitches to be pronounced. She had come, she told me, with a whisper and wink, to take me away and better me. [Queenie]

PAGE 212. "Bernard, I've enjoyed our little trips but I don't think we should see each other any more." I said it on a park bench, as a drizzle of rain was just starting to polka-dot his coat. Like a baby who's just been slapped but doesn't know it smarts yet, it happened ever so slowly. His face went from plain-day, through quizzical, then headlong into hurt. I never thought Bernard could be caught by feelings but there they were. Unmistakable it was, the quivering lip, the watering eye. He was about to cry. It was the most exciting thing he'd ever done. [Queenie]

PAGE 222. Bernard became almost animated talking with the next-door neighbor, Mr Todd. "They'd be happier among their own kind," he said. The two of them, arms folded, heads practically touching and shaking sombrely. "Putting them here really isn't doing anyone any good." I thought it must be Hitler outside our door. Or perhaps the entire Third Reich was moving in down our street. There was such a rumpus ... But it wasn't an invasion – it was a sadder sight than that. It was a family. A mother wearing a brown coat with one sleeve hanging off, carrying a baby wrapped in a shawl made of an old sheet. Her face not so much blank but unreadable as a corpse. And struggling behind her were four kids. [Queenie]

PAGE 237. It was my fault that Bernard volunteered for the RAF before waiting to be asked. Men not in uniform began to look out of place in streets rolling in blue and khaki ... He had to join up ... Bernard was to become part of their fighting machine – they were sending him overseas. Mr Todd slapped his back, saying, "Good show, Bernard, good man" ... And when I talked about him I plumped almost as proud as Auntie Dorothy ... I swear his shoulders got broader, his hands more manly with every leave. Even the back of his neck looked fearless with the collar of his RAF blues pressing against it. [Queenie]

PAGE 281, 282. We were packed like cattle on to the train in Bombay ... Hundreds of troops. We walked three abreast into the station but were quickly outnumbered. Brown people all around. At my back, at my front, under my arms. Hands out. White palms begging ...

... The station was familiar. A concrete building with vaulting roof. Could have been back home – St. Pancras or Liverpool Street.

There was even a man in a black bowler hat bobbing through the crowd. Looked like Pa on his way to work. Except he wore a long shirt and his legs were wrapped in baggy white cotton pants.

... The train might have been in Bombay but the footplate I stuck my boot on said it was made in Crewe. [Bernard]

PAGE 300. Then we got the order to move. Everyone cheered. Only to find we were moving nearer to Burma. Going the wrong way, the chaps shouted.

... Top brass insisted POWs should get home first ... They came through the camp on their way to Bombay. I gave one of them my chocolate ration ... He'd flown a glider behind the Jap lines. Been in their hands for nearly two years. His bones jangled inside his skin like coins in a bag. Could almost see the squares of chocolate passing down him. Had to watch as he clutched his stomach ... Too rich for him ... "Sorry," he said, "what a waste." Every man was happy to stand aside to let these flimsy scraps of Englishmen get home. What race of people could watch flesh wither on a man until he was no more than a framework? Left me proud to belong to a civilization where even the most aggrieved was held back from raising a hand to our Japanese prisoners. [Bernard]

PAGE 331. She got his body back – in one piece, whole, hardly touched. A body that defecated every time a door closed too loudly ... "Your father's lost his mind," she told me. And I, aged eight, hoped if someone found it they'd bring it home for him. [Bernard]

PAGE 332. She had a big house and a small pension ... The handed-down silver cruet that sat on the parlour table disappeared, one piece at a time. So did the rings on her fingers. Except her wedding band, which she twirled every time she watched my father in his garden. She let rooms in the house. Spent her time chasing rent and morals up and down the staircase. [Bernard]

PAGE 340, 341. Didn't take long. Yelled out (I admit). Ejaculation was a blessed release, like lowering myself into a cool bath ... A few moments of peace before I realised I still had her hair wrapped tight in my fist ... I soon let go and she quickly pulled herself away from me ... And only then did I see that she was nothing but a girl ... Fourteen or even twelve. A small girl ...

What would Queenie think of her husband now? Trousers round my ankles in a brothel, defiling someone's daughter. "Is this what the war's done for you?" she'd say. This war hadn't made me a hero. It had brought me to my knees. [Bernard]

PAGE 364. Hortense was huddle up on the floor over a pan on the wretched gas ring. Her young back should not have been folded like a crone's – it should have been standing haughty and straight at a good cook-er. But, come, like watching a right-hand person use their left, when she was cooking, she make every movement a torture to behold. [Gilbert]

PAGE 372. Anyone hearing Gilbert Joseph speak would know without hesitation that this man was not English. No matter that he is dressed in his best suit, his hair greased, his fingernails clean, he talked (and walked) in a rough Jamaican way. Whereas I, since arriving in this country, had determined to speak in an English manner ...

...To prove practice makes perfect, on two occasions a shopkeeper had brought me the item requested without repetition from me. With thanks to that impeccable English evidenced on my wireless, I was understood easily. [Hortense]

PAGE 374. "Good day," I said.

Two dropped their heads returning to their business as if I had not spoken, leaving just an older woman to ask, "Yes, do you want something?" This woman smiled on me – her countenance gleaming with so much joy that I could do nothing but return the welcome ..

... "I am a teacher," I said, intending to carry on with some further explanation ... Having composed myself I began again. "I am a teacher and I understand this is the place at which I should present myself for a position in that particular profession." Through this woman's warm smile I detected a little confusion. Too well bred to say "What?" she looked a quizzical eye on me which shouted the word just as audibly. [Hortense]

PAGE 376. "It doesn't matter that you were a teacher in Jamaica ... you will not be allowed to teach here ... Take thee back ..." Her smile was stale as a gargoyle ...

"Must I go back to a college?"

"Really, miss, I have just explained everything to you. You do speak English? Have you not understood me? It's quite simple ..."

As I stood she rolled her eyes with the other women in the room. But I paid them no mind. I fixed my hat straight on my head and adjusted my gloves. "Thank you and good day," I called to them all, as I opened the door ... and walked through. Suddenly everything was dark ... Only when my foot kicked against a bucket did I realise I had walked into a cupboard ... [Hortense]

PAGE 383, 384. "You like the palace?" I asked her.

Stiff and composed she replied, "I have seen it in books."

"People always stare on us, Hortense," I told her.

"And I pay them no mind," she snapped back to me.

"Good, because you know what? The King has the same problem." But her nose had risen into the air and I feared I was losing her once more. I put my elbow out to her. "Come let us stroll like the King and Queen down the mall." [Gilbert]

PAGE 395, 396. "Mrs Bligh, are you with child?"

Once the bandage was fully discarded it was plain as a drink of water ...

... "there's no time ... I know it's coming." Once again the pain was scorching her face crimson. It was not in my experience, giving birth. I had watched chickens, of course, laying their eggs, but none of them had ever required my assistance ...

... "Don't worry, I know what to do." She struggled with a little giggle, "It'll be like Gone With The Wind." [Hortense]

PAGE 398, 399. I lifted the baby carefully so she might see. She held out her arms. The slimy purple pink of a robust earthworm, with skin smeared in blood and wrinkled as the day it would die, and yet still Mrs Bligh's eyes alighted on this grumpy-faced child and saw it as someone she could love. This was truly the miracle to behold ... And luckily my dress had remained clean ...

... I had no time for this reverie for the room was cold, the mother gone fool-fool and the baby naked. Every blanket had slipped to the floor in all the confusion. Bending to retrieve them at the foot of the bed, I found myself awkward by the feet of Mrs Bligh. When, all at once, Mrs Bligh's private part let forth a burp then spat out on to the lap of my best white wedding dress a bloody-soaked lump of her insides ...

Soaking pink with the bloody splattered tissue, my poor dress wept. [Hortense]

PAGE 404. Come, I finally get it. She had weighed up the evidence and reached the same conclusion as the fool husband. The brown baby in Queenie's arms must be the child she had for me. Cha! Am I the only black man in this world? Why everyone look to me? I have been back in England for only seven months. Why no one think to use their fingers to count out that before they accuse? [Gilbert]

PAGE 418. I had got used to folding myself up on to the armchair to go to bed. My limbs had become collapsible. There was no winged creature that could tuck and bend itself away as neatly as I. I might have been crumpled as a moth from its cocoon every morning, but with the light, blood soon pumped through me to make me a man again. And under my big blanket I was snug as a bug. Like every night before, I turned out the light and wished Hortense pleasant dreams. But on this night, when all was dark and quiet, I heard her softly spoken voice say, "Gilbert." [Gilbert]

PAGE 424. Bernard wanted me and him to move to the suburbs. A nice house, semi-detached with a rose garden out the front and a small lawn at the back. "Manageable" was the word he used. Not like this house with its memories, its prospect haunting his every thought. He was wanting a new start. Didn't they all, those fighting men? I mean, they'd won. They deserved something out of it, surely. What else was the victory for? Bernard was never half so interesting as when he was at his war. He thought I'd find his story ... shocking. But no. I just wanted to laugh. Shout loud and congratulate him on failing to be dull for once in his life. I know two wrongs will never make a right but at least now we could stand up straight in each other's company. Even if it was caught in the clinch of two skeletons in a cupboard. [Queenie]

PAGE 432. "If I gave him to an orphanage," I carried on, "I'd never know about him. Never. And he wouldn't know how much I loved him. And how all I wanted was to be a good mother to him." They were just staring at me. I must have looked – no, I was – pathetic. "You might let me know how he was getting on. You might write to me and tell me. I know it's a lot to ask." [Queenie]

PAGE 433. I never dreamed England would be like this. Come, in what crazed reverie would a white Englishwoman be kneeling before me yearning for me to take her black child? There was no dream I could conceive so fanciful ... Could we take her newly-born son and call him our own? Not even Celia Langley, with her nose in the air and her head in a cloud, would have imagined something so preposterous of this Mother Country. [Hortense]

PAGE 435. "Listen to me, man, we both just finish fighting a war – a bloody war – for the better world we wan' see. And on the same side – you and me. We both look on other men to see enemy. You and me, fighting for empire, fighting for peace. But still, after all that we suffer together, you wan' tell me I am worthless and you are not. Am I to be the servant and you are the master for all time? No. Stop this, man. Stop it now. We can work together, Mr Bligh. You no see? We must. Or else you just gonna fight me till the end?"

...I realised that Gilbert Joseph, my husband, was a man of class, a man of character, a man of intelligence. Noble in a way that would some day make him a legend. "Gilbert Joseph," everyone would shout. "Have you heard about Gilbert Joseph?" [Hortense]

PAGE 438. I tapped gently three times. There was no reply ... She was there – I knew. "Goodbye, Queenie," I called, but still she did not come.

...Gilbert ... took the baby from me. I adjusted my hat in case it sagged in the damp air and left me looking comical. A curtain at the window moved – just a little but enough for me to know it was not the breeze. But I paid it no mind as I pulled my back up and straightened my coat against the cold. [Hortense]

ACKNOWLEDGEMENTS

ACKNOWLEDGEMENTS

Allardice, Lisa. "I've just had my own Halle Berry moment." *The Globe and Mail,* Toronto: January, 2005.

Andrea Levy. "Levy - Every inch an Englishwoman." Interview by Jasper Gerard. www.timesonline.co.uk. June 2005.

Bauer, Carlene. *Being Black and British.* www.books.guardian.co.uk., April, 2005.

Birmingham.gov.uk. "Birmingham's Post War Black Immigrants."

Burns, Carole. "Off the Page: Andrea Levy." washingtonpost.com, June 2004.

Ferguson, James. *A Traveller's History of the Caribbean.* New York: Interlink Books, An Imprint of Interlink Publishing Group, Inc., 1999.

Hickman, Christie. "Andrea Levy: Under the skin of history." independent.co.uk. June 2005.

Marshall, P.J. (editor) "British Empire." Cambridge Illustrated History. Cambridge University Press, Cambridge: 1996.

Shea, Renee H., "Already Famous." *Poets & Writers Magazine,* New York: May/June 2005.

Sherlock, Philip and Bennett, Hazel. *The Story of the Jamaican People.* Jamaica: Ian Randle Publishers Ltd., Kingston, 1998.